Terry
Border

BIG BROTHER
PEANUT
BUTTER

PHILOMEL BOOKS

PHILOMEL BOOKS

an imprint of Penguin Random House LLC
375 Hudson Street
New York, NY 10014

Library of Congress Cataloging-in-Publication Data
Names: Border, Terry, 1965– author.
Title: Big brother Peanut Butter / Terry Border.
Description: New York, NY : Philomel Books, [2018]
Summary: When Peanut Butter learns that his parents are expecting a baby, he begins asking his friends and neighbors how to be the perfect big brother.
Identifiers: LCCN 2017050523 | ISBN 9781524740061 (hardcover) | ISBN 9781524740092 (e-book)
Subjects: | CYAC: Brothers—Fiction. | Food—Fiction.
Classification: LCC PZ7.B64832 Big 2018 | DDC [E]—dc23
LC record available at https://lccn.loc.gov/2017050523
Manufactured in China by RR Donnelley Asia Printing Solutions Ltd.
ISBN 9781524740061
1 3 5 7 9 10 8 6 4 2

Edited by Jill Santopolo.
Design by Ellice M. Lee.
Text set in Hank BT.

The art was done by manipulating and photographing three-dimensional objects.

To my brother,
Duane. He used to
be my little brother,
but now I'm his
little brother.

Early one morning, Peanut Butter's parents called him into the kitchen to tell him some great news.

"Guess what! You're going to be a big brother," said his mom.

A big brother? Peanut Butter had never been a big brother before.

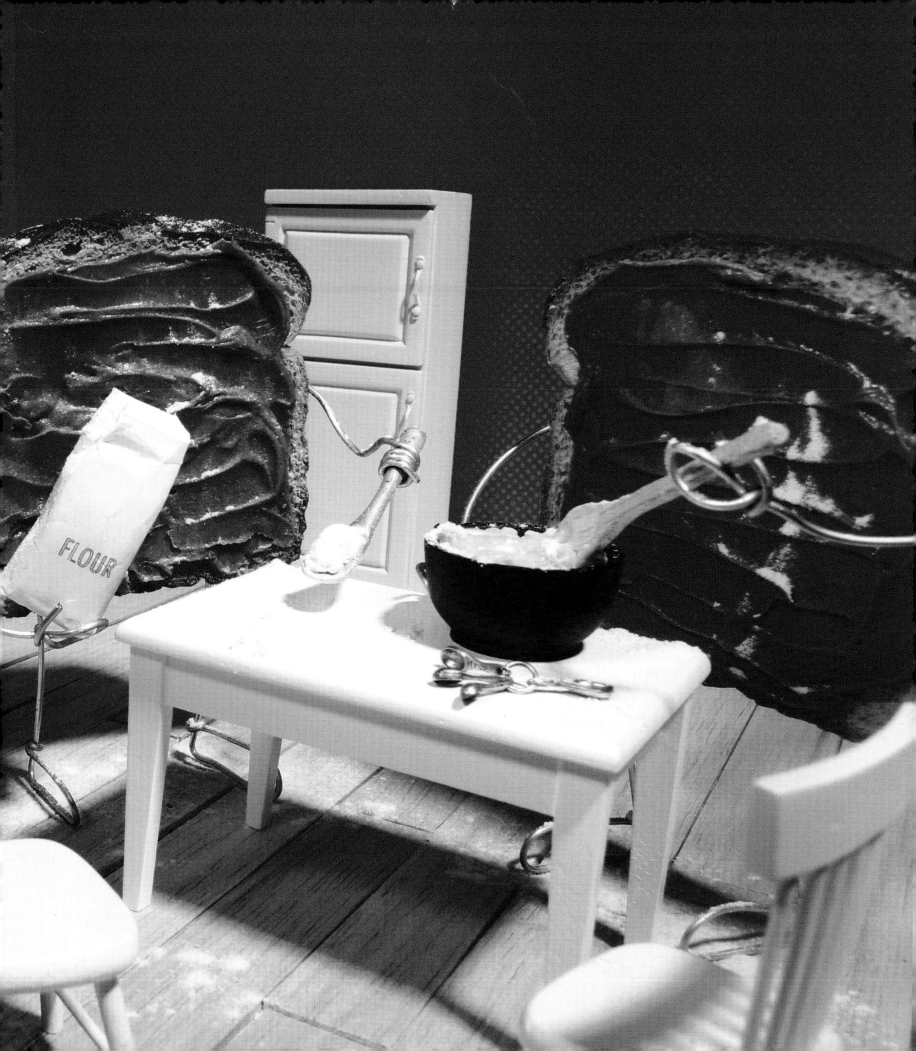

"Is it hard?" Peanut Butter asked.
"To be a big brother?"

"Easy as Pie," said his dad.
"You should ask her about it."

Peanut Butter thought that was a
great idea, so he went to find her.
Apple Pie had two baby brothers:
Blueberry and Cherry.

Once he found her, Peanut Butter said:

"My parents had one kid, now they're having another,
and I want to be a perfect big brother!
It'll take lots of practice, but I hope to see
that I need to act just like a good . . . Pie."

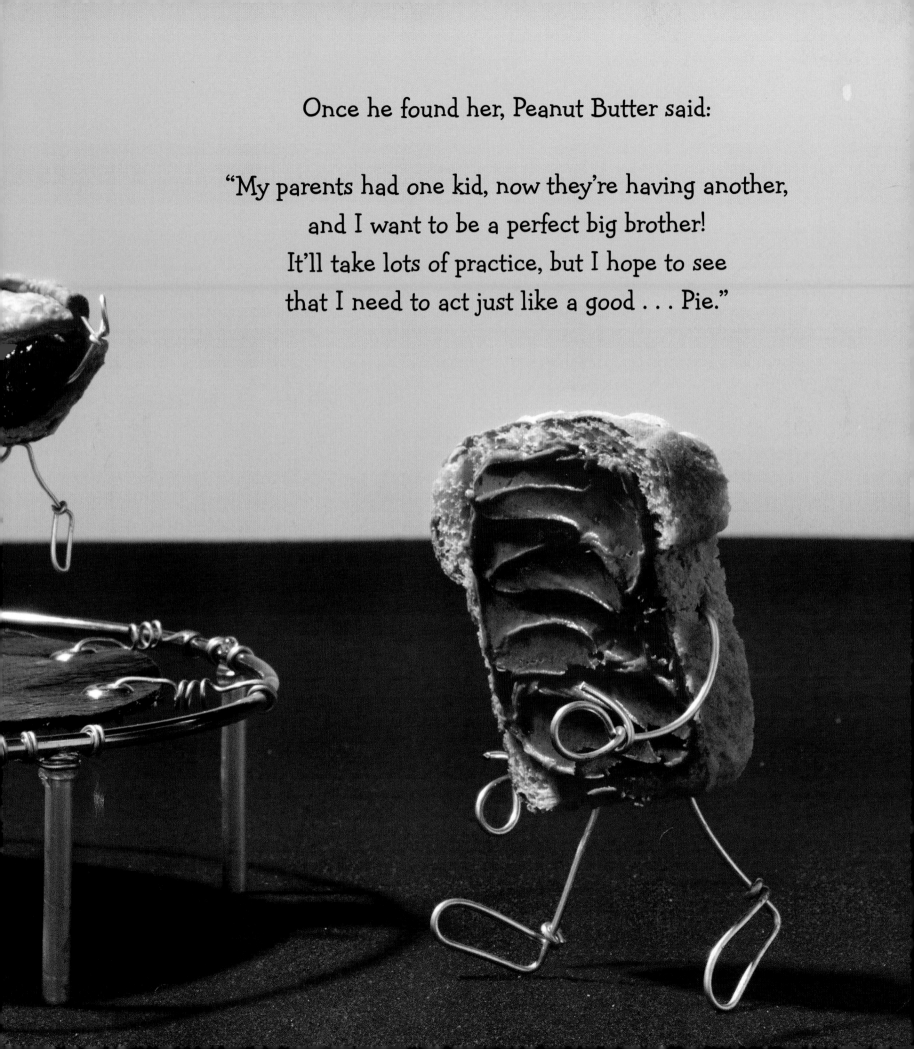

"Why do you say that?" asked Apple Pie.
"Well, you make being a big sister look
so easy, I thought I should act like you," said
Peanut Butter.

Apple Pie laughed. "Don't be nervous.
You'll figure it out."
"Don't be nervous?" asked Peanut
Butter. "That gives me an idea!"

He found the kid he was looking for at the swings.

"My parents had one kid, now they're having another,
and I want to be a perfect big brother!
It'll take lots of practice, but I hope to see
that I need to act just like a good . . . Cucumber!"

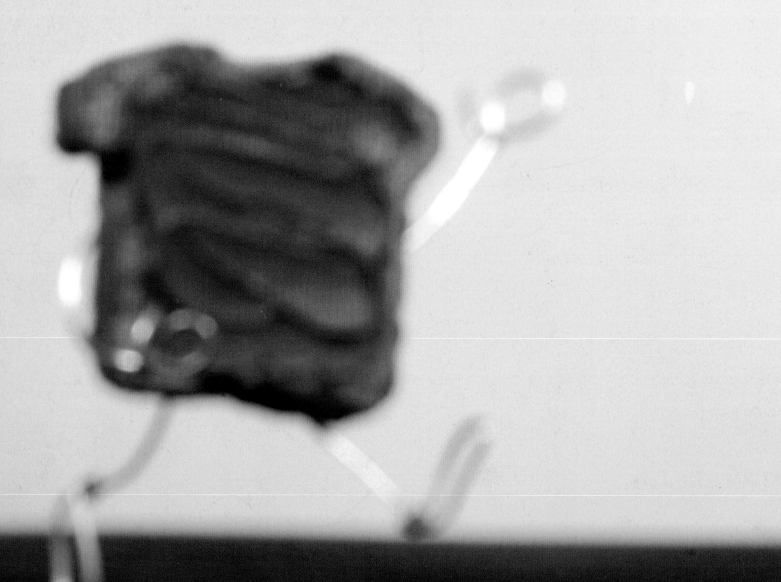

"Hmm?" asked Cucumber.

"I don't want to be nervous—I want to be cool as a Cucumber, just like you!" said Peanut Butter. "Who wouldn't want to have a cool big brother?"

"Well, I am a super-cool dude," said Cucumber. "And so's my kid brother."

Cucumber's brother, Dill Pickle, smiled up at him. Then he looked at Peanut Butter. "My brother's so cool, he pushes me really high. Want to try?"

So Peanut Butter went over and pushed Dill's swing super high.

"I'll see you both later," he said. "I need to ask someone else a question."

Peanut Butter had to wait in a line to talk to the next person on his list. After a while, he got impatient, so he shouted:

"My parents had one kid, now they're having another, and I want to be a perfect big brother! It'll take lots of practice, but I hope to see that I need to act just like a good . . . Cheese!"

"You've got to wait your turn. We're all here to see Big Cheese. He's very important!" said a pair of Pears who were in line already.

"I know," said Peanut Butter. "That's why I want to be more like him. Who wouldn't want an important big brother?"

Peanut Butter turned and saw a little Cheese standing in line behind him.

"Hi there," said Peanut Butter. "Who are you?"

"I'm Big Cheese's little sister, Pepper Jack," she said. "I'm waiting here because my kite's stuck in a tree. He said he'll get it down for me when he's done."

"I can help," said Peanut Butter.

When the kite was unstuck, Peanut Butter's best friend, Jelly, came over.

"What's going on?" she asked.

"I've been trying to figure out how to be a perfect big brother all day," said Peanut Butter. "I think I need to be calm and cool and important . . . but I'm not sure I'm any of those things."

"Hmm," Jelly said. "I don't have any little brothers or sisters, but I do have a big brother myself. He's a good big brother even though he's not any of the things you were trying to be."

"He isn't?" Peanut Butter asked.

"Nope," said Jelly. "He does a lot of other things, but the most important thing he does is love me. And I love him right back."

"I think I understand now," he said. Apple Pie had always been calm. Cucumber had always been cool. Big Cheese had always been important. They didn't have to change when they became a big sister or brother. They just had to love their little brothers and sisters. Peanut Butter could do that!

"My parents had one kid, now they're having another,
and I want to be a perfect big brother!
It'll take lots of practice, but I hope to see
that I need to act just like a good . . . ME!"

"Yes!" said Jelly. "I have a feeling you know how
to do that."

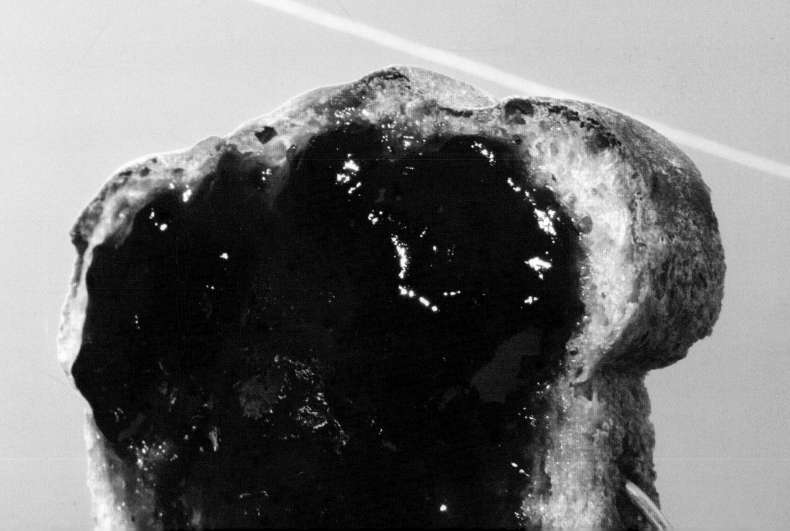

Jelly walked with Peanut Butter as he headed home.
As they got closer to his house, they heard a baby crying.
Then they heard two babies crying. Was it twins?
Then it sounded like three babies. Then four! Then five!

Peanut Butter and Jelly rushed inside
the house to see what was going on.

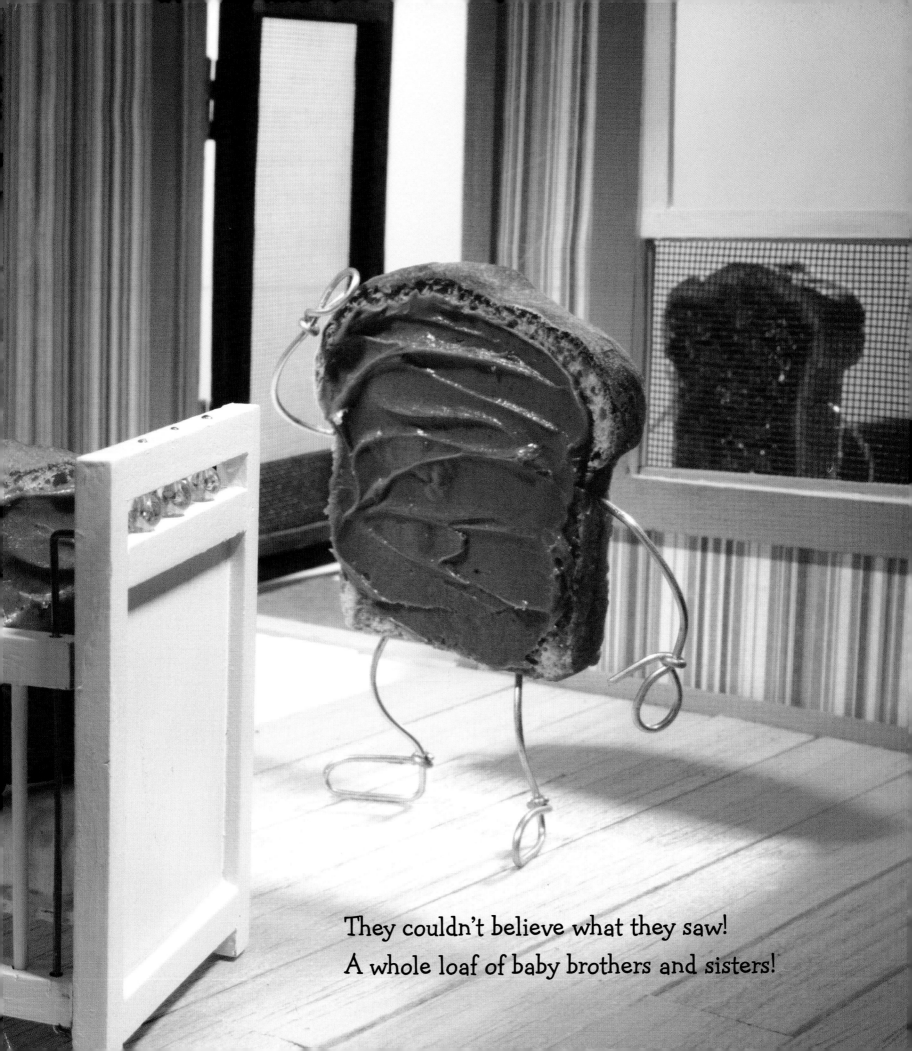

They couldn't believe what they saw!
A whole loaf of baby brothers and sisters!

His mother looked over at Peanut Butter and said:

"We had one kid, now we have many others,
and they'll need the love of their big older brother!
It may take some practice, but I think we'll see
that we'll make a big happy bread family!"